It's the Great Pumpkin, Charlie Brown™

BY CHARLES M. SCHULZ

RP|KIDS

PHILADELPHIA • LONDON

ISBN 978-0-7624-3302-5

Text adapted by Megan E. Bryant
Art adapted by Tom Brannon
Design by Frances J. Soo Ping Chow

Running Press Book Publishers
2300 Chestnut Street
Philadelphia, PA 19103-4371

Visit us on the web!
www.runningpress.com
www.Snoopy.com

Charlie Brown was raking leaves. Lucy was holding a football. And Linus was inspecting the pumpkin patch.

It could only mean one thing: Halloween was almost here!

Back inside, Linus started writing his yearly letter to the Great Pumpkin.
"Dear Great Pumpkin. I'm looking forward to your arrival on Halloween night.
I hope you will bring me lots of presents."

"Who are you writing to, Linus?" asked Charlie Brown.

"The Great Pumpkin!" Linus replied. "On Halloween night, the Great Pumpkin rises out of his pumpkin patch and flies through the air with his bag of toys for all the children."

"You must be crazy," Charlie Brown said.

The rest of the Peanuts gang thought that Linus was crazy, too. But Charlie Brown's little sister, Sally, was very interested in the Great Pumpkin—and in Linus.

"Wouldn't you like to sit with me in the pumpkin patch on Halloween night and wait for the Great Pumpkin?" Linus asked.

"Oh, I'd love to, Linus!" replied Sally, batting her eyes.

When the mail came, there was a surprise for Charlie Brown. "I got an invitation to a Halloween party!" he exclaimed.

"Is the invitation to Violet's party?" asked Lucy. "If you got an invitation, it was a mistake! There were two lists—one to invite, and one not to invite."

Charlie Brown was embarrassed. But he decided to go to the Halloween party anyway. He could hardly wait!

On Halloween night, Charlie Brown met up with his friends. Lucy wore a witch mask. Charlie Brown's ghost costume looked a little funny. It was covered in big black eyeholes because he'd gotten a little carried away with the scissors!

Just then, Snoopy passed by wearing a long red scarf, goggles, and an aviator cap.

"It's the World War One Flying Ace," said Charlie Brown.

"Now I've heard everything," Lucy sighed. "All right, everybody. Let's go trick or treating and then to Violet's for the big party."

But the World War I Flying Ace ignored her. He had to go on an important mission!

The World War I Flying Ace climbed into the cockpit of his Sopwith Camel airplane. It was up to him to find the Red Baron and bring him down! He flew through the sky, firing at his targets.

Suddenly, the Sopwith Camel was hit! The plane started smoking and spiraling through the air. It landed with a loud crash.

Now the World War I Flying Ace would have to continue his mission on foot. He crept through the French countryside, slinking through the bushes and wading through a lake.

As the kids passed the pumpkin patch, they saw Linus waiting for the Great Pumpkin. "You blockhead! You're going to miss all the fun just like last year!" Lucy groaned.

Sally was torn. Should she go trick or treating or wait for the Great Pumpkin with Linus? Suddenly, she ran back to the pumpkin patch.

"I'm glad you came back, Sally," Linus said. "Each year the Great Pumpkin rises out of the pumpkin patch that he thinks is the most sincere."

At the first house they reached, everyone yelled, "Tricks or treats, money or eats!" Then they compared their haul.

"I got five pieces of candy!" yelled Lucy.

"I got a chocolate bar!" Violet cried.

"I got a quarter," Patty said happily.

Charlie Brown peered into his bag. "I got a rock."

And that was what happened at every single house. While the rest of his friends got treats like candy bars, cookies, gum, and popcorn balls, Charlie Brown's bag filled up with rocks!

"Come on, let's get going," Lucy said in a bossy voice. "It's time for the Halloween party."

As the kids passed the pumpkin patch again, they laughed at Linus and Sally.

"The Great Pumpkin will be here! Linus knows what he's talking about!" hollered Sally. Then she turned to Linus. "All right, where is he?"

"He'll be here," Linus promised.

"I hope so," Sally replied grumpily. "Just think of all the fun we're missing!"

But at the Halloween party, Charlie Brown didn't think Sally and Linus were missing anything. The other kids wanted him to model for their jack-o-lantern— so they drew a big pumpkin-face on the back of his head!

Then the kids bobbed for apples. But when Lucy nabbed an apple, she was disgusted to find the World War I Flying Ace on the other side of it!

"My lips touched dog lips!" she howled. "Bleah . . . augh!"

The World War I Flying Ace was insulted. He slunk out the door to continue his mission.

"If anyone had told me I'd be waiting in a pumpkin patch on Halloween night, I'd have said they were crazy," Sally grumbled.

Then she and Linus heard a rustling noise. A dark figure appeared before them.

"What's that?" Linus exclaimed. "It's the Great Pumpkin! He's rising up out of the pumpkin patch!"

In all the excitement, Linus fainted. But it wasn't the Great Pumpkin at all! It was the World War I Flying Ace on his imaginary mission!

"What happened? Did he leave us any toys?" Linus asked as he sat up.

Sally was furious. "I was robbed!" she yelled. "Halloween is over and I've missed it!" She stormed out of the pumpkin patch, leaving Linus alone to wait for the Great Pumpkin.

In the middle of the night, Lucy woke up and realized Linus was still waiting for the Great Pumpkin. She found him asleep, shivering under his blanket. Lucy brought her brother home and tucked him into bed.

"Well, another Halloween has come and gone," Charlie Brown said the next day. "Don't take it too hard that the Great Pumpkin never showed up."

"Just wait till next year, Charlie Brown! I'll find a pumpkin patch that is real sincere, and I'll sit in that pumpkin patch until the Great Pumpkin appears!" Linus exclaimed.